Down Dairy Farm Road

C. L. G. Martin ◆ *Illustrated by* Diane Dawson Hearn

Macmillan Publishing Company   New York
Maxwell Macmillan Canada   Toronto
Maxwell Macmillan International   New York   Oxford   Singapore   Sydney

Library of Congress Cataloging-in-Publication Data
Martin, C. L. G. Down Dairy Farm Road / C. L. G. Martin ; illustrated by Diane Dawson Hearn. — 1st ed.   p.   cm.
Summary: Making the rounds with her veterinarian grandfather helps Junie Mae come to terms with her envious feelings toward a
wealthier little girl.   ISBN 0-02-762450-1   [1. Grandfathers—Fiction.   2. Veterinarians—Fiction.   3. Domestic animals—
Fiction.   4. Farm life—Fiction.]   I. Hearn, Diane Dawson, ill.   II. Title.   PZ7.M356776Do   1994   [E]—dc20
92-42848

In warm remembrance of Grandpa
—*C. L. G. M.*

To my sister, Daddle's June Bug
—*D. D. H.*

Junie Mae studied her reflection in the birdbath. "Lucinda Bodine says my hair is straight and sorry as an old rope, Grandpa. She says anybody who's *anybody* has their hair permed at Miss Carlene's Beauty Boutique."

"You know we can't afford a visit to the beauty parlor, June Bug."

Junie Mae sighed. Life hadn't been the same since Lucinda Bodine had moved to Dairy Farm Road.

"Come along on my rounds, Junie Mae. Mrs. Olsen has a new litter of kittens." Grandpa lifted her into the grocery wagon behind his big black bag, and together they set off down Dairy Farm Road.

Kittens, Junie Mae thought, were probably the only thing that could take her mind off that uppity Lucinda Bodine and her beauty parlor hair.

"Hello, Junie Mae," Mrs. Olsen shouted. "I'll bet you're here to see my kittens."

A golden colt broke away from the blue-ribbon horses in Mrs. Olsen's corral, greeting Grandpa like a friendly puppy. Junie Mae stared at his tail. It was woven into a big, beautiful cinnamon braid. "Horsehair that's nicer than mine," she mumbled, shuffling across the barnyard.

From the dark, hay-strewn barn came a chorus of squeaky, lonely meows.

"Junie Mae," Mrs. Olsen called from the barn door, "would you feed them for me?"

Junie Mae knew how to mother kittens. She dipped her finger in the pan of warm milk and rubbed it on their lips until they got a taste. Before long, five little heads circled the pan, splashing, choking, gurgling, and occasionally blowing milk bubbles through their noses.

"You've got the touch with animals, just like your grandpa," declared Mrs. Olsen. "Would you like to farm the kittens out for me? You can keep what you make off them."

"Really?" Five kittens at a dollar apiece would be enough for a perm at Miss Carlene's Beauty Boutique. Wouldn't *that* show that snooty Lucinda Bodine!

Junie Mae settled into the grocery wagon with the basket of squirming kittens safely in her lap. Kittens need names, she decided, important, respectable names to make them feel special.

"Can this one be Dwight, Grandpa?"

"I don't think President Eisenhower would mind, June Bug."

"Good," Junie Mae said, scratching Dwight behind the ears.

"We could call that little climber Edmund Hillary after that fellow who just climbed Mount Everest," suggested Grandpa.

"You can be Elizabeth, after the new queen," Junie Mae said to the little calico. "And you," she continued, addressing the tiger-striped gray, "are Willie Mays." The little black tom meowed for attention, but at the moment, Junie Mae couldn't think of another special name.

"A real Who's Who of Green Valley cats." Grandpa nodded approvingly. "Next patient is Mr. Anderson's cow," he said as he pulled the wagon back onto Dairy Farm Road.

"Hi, Mr. Anderson. Do you need a kitten?"

"I could use a good mouser for the barn, Junie Mae. How much?"

"One dollar."

"Gee, that's a little steep for me this month. Maybe next time."

Next time? Junie Mae lay back in the wagon and stared at the clouds. They looked like Lucinda Bodine's beauty parlor curls.

Grandpa plopped a gunnysack of sweet corn into the wagon. "Crystal's calf is coming soon," he said.

"Good." Junie Mae was anxious to go. She waved good-bye to Mr. Anderson, and off they went down Dairy Farm Road, to tend to the Kelseys' bull.

"Hi, Doc. Hi, Junie Mae." Jack and Zack Kelsey ran toward them. "Caesar's in the barn, Doc," said Zack.

"Oooooo, kittens!" cried Jack and Zack together.

Junie Mae liked boys who weren't ashamed to cuddle kittens. "Only one dollar," she said encouragingly.

Jack and Zack put the kittens back in their basket.

"Caesar's good as new," announced Grandpa, loading a bushel of beans and two acorn squash into the wagon.

Junie Mae leaned against the silken corn tassels. Even corn has prettier hair than I do, she thought miserably, and off they went down Dairy Farm Road. The wagon was getting very crowded.

"One more stop," said Grandpa. "Mrs. Whittlesey's goose."

"Mrs. Whittlesey? If we go to Mrs. Whittlesey's, we have to go right past Lucinda Bodine's house!" Junie Mae groaned. How could she pass Lucinda Bodine's fancy house and her shiny red car in a rickety grocery wagon packed with corn and beans and squash?

Lucinda Bodine's brand-new bicycle lay in a muddy ditch on top of a pair of roller skates. Junie Mae shook her head.

"Yoo-hoo! Is that you, Junie Mae?"

Junie Mae ducked behind the sweet corn. Her face grew warmer than the dirt on Dairy Farm Road.

Lucinda Bodine skipped down the drive, Miss Carlene's beauty parlor curls bouncing smartly around her head. "Why, Junie Mae, whatever are you doing in that dirty old grocery wagon? Ooooooo, kittens! Are they for sale? I want them!"

"*All* of them?"

"I'll go get the money from my daddy," Lucinda cried excitedly.

This was too good to be true. Lucinda Bodine was going to pay for Junie Mae's perm.

Junie Mae looked into the jiggling, jumping kitten basket. Ten tiny blue eyes looked trustingly back. "They're not for sale," she heard herself suddenly say. How could she sell kittens to a person who left her brand-new bicycle and her roller skates in the mud?

"Well, fine!" snapped Lucinda Bodine. "I didn't want those sorry-looking kittens, anyway!" She stomped back up the drive, her beauty parlor curls flapping angrily in all directions.

Grandpa winked a secret wink, and off they went down Dairy Farm Road.

Junie Mae stroked her kittens fondly. Mrs. Whittlesey lived all alone. Maybe she'd buy one.

Honk! Honk! Honk!

"Goose patrol!" yelled Grandpa, and Junie Mae swung her bare feet quickly into the wagon, upsetting the kitten basket.

"Whoa!" called Mrs. Whittlesey sternly. The angry geese retreated, forming a protective circle around their gray-haired mistress.

Junie Mae rounded up her scattered kittens. Where was Edmund?

"Oh, my!" Mrs. Whittlesey dashed to the edge of her porch and plucked the dangling Edmund from a crab apple tree. "Aren't you the sweetest, snuggliest thing," she cooed, and Edmund purred contentedly.

"Kittens are a lot more cuddly than those dumb geese," Junie Mae whispered, and Grandpa agreed.

Junie Mae climbed into the wagon, balancing the kitten basket under Mrs. Whittlesey's fresh apple pie. "Will you keep Edmund for me, Mrs. Whittlesey? He needs a good home."

"I surely will, Junie Mae. Thank you."

Grandpa patted Junie Mae's head. "You have a good heart, June Bug."

Junie Mae sighed. A good heart and no money to perm the sorriest, straightest hair on Dairy Farm Road.

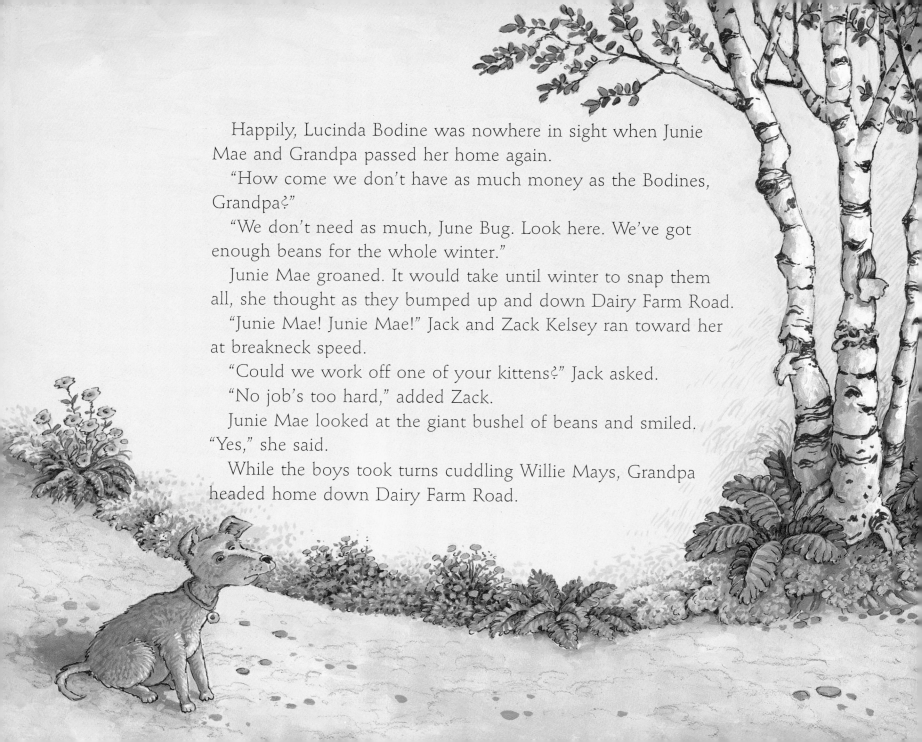

Happily, Lucinda Bodine was nowhere in sight when Junie Mae and Grandpa passed her home again.

"How come we don't have as much money as the Bodines, Grandpa?"

"We don't need as much, June Bug. Look here. We've got enough beans for the whole winter."

Junie Mae groaned. It would take until winter to snap them all, she thought as they bumped up and down Dairy Farm Road.

"Junie Mae! Junie Mae!" Jack and Zack Kelsey ran toward her at breakneck speed.

"Could we work off one of your kittens?" Jack asked.

"No job's too hard," added Zack.

Junie Mae looked at the giant bushel of beans and smiled. "Yes," she said.

While the boys took turns cuddling Willie Mays, Grandpa headed home down Dairy Farm Road.

"Doc! Doc! Come quick!" Mr. Anderson yelled, disappearing into his barn.

Junie Mae felt afraid as Grandpa ran after him.

"Sometimes calves need a little help getting born," Mrs. Anderson explained. "Everything will be fine now that your grandpa's here."

Dwight sneezed, and Mrs. Anderson chuckled.

"Would you like to keep him?" Junie Mae asked.

"Why, thank you, Junie Mae."

"It's a girl!" called Mr. Anderson from the barn.

"Yahoo!" cried Mrs. Anderson. "What did I tell you, Junie Mae?"

Junie Mae climbed proudly into the wagon with the big, black bag, the squash, the beans, the corn, the pie, and the two remaining kittens. Mrs. Anderson stuffed a quart of pickles between Junie Mae's knees, and Mr. Anderson promised free milk all month.

"Appreciate it," said Grandpa, and off they went down Dairy Farm Road.

"Hi, Mrs. Olsen," Junie Mae called excitedly. "I gave away three of the kittens."

"Good job, Junie Mae. I think I'll take the little calico back. I missed her. Now, I want to give you something for all your trouble. What'll it be?"

Junie Mae pointed shyly at the golden colt with the cinnamon tail. "Would you fix my hair like that?"

"Hop on my lap and I'll see what I can do."

Mrs. Olsen hummed cheerfully as she worked. "Hard to believe how sick that colt was only a few weeks ago, eh, Doc? Junie Mae, your grandpa slept out in that barn two whole nights, nursing Shooting Star."

Junie Mae smiled at her grandpa.

When Mrs. Olsen had finished, Grandpa stared at Junie Mae. "Is that really you, June Bug?" he asked.

Mrs. Olsen held up a mirror.

"Real blue-ribbon hair," proclaimed Grandpa.

Junie Mae blushed. She hardly recognized her hair, gathered into a neat, thick braid and topped with a blue satin ribbon. She looked positively…eight…maybe nine.

Junie Mae hugged Mrs. Olsen quickly and wiggled into the loaded wagon. The little black tom pulled on her new braid. "Hey!" She laughed. "I owe you a name, don't I? Well, now I have the best name for you."

"What would that be, Junie Mae?" asked Grandpa.

"I'm gonna call him Doc."

Grandpa smiled. "Thank you, June Bug. You are going to be a great comfort to me in my old age."

"Yes, I am," said Junie Mae respectfully. "Can I keep him?"

Grandpa nodded.

Just then, a shiny red car pulled alongside the wagon.

"Hi, there, Junie Mae," called Mr. Bodine. "We've got a new patient for you, Doc."

Lucinda Bodine grinned and held up a luxurious, long-haired, store-bought cat that promptly bit her finger. "Youch!" she shrieked.

"See you, Doc," said Mr. Bodine. "You look very pretty today, Junie Mae."

Junie Mae waved good-bye, but Lucinda Bodine didn't even turn her pouty face around. Doc meowed for attention, and Junie Mae rubbed his tummy.

Dairy Farm Road felt warm and friendly on her dusty bare feet.